OINK

Arthur Geisert

Houghton Mifflin Company

Boston

For Tony and Leona Meier
Faulk County, South Dakota

Library of Congress Cataloging-in-Publication Data

Geisert, Arthur.
  Oink / Arthur Geisert.
     p. cm.
  Summary: When their mother falls asleep, the baby pigs sneak away,
get into big trouble, and must be rescued.
  ISBN 0-395-55329-6
  [1. Pigs—Fiction.]   I. Title.
PZ7.G272401   1991   90-46123
[E]—dc20   CIP
                 AC

Printed in the United States of America

HOR   10 9 8 7 6 5 4 3

OINK

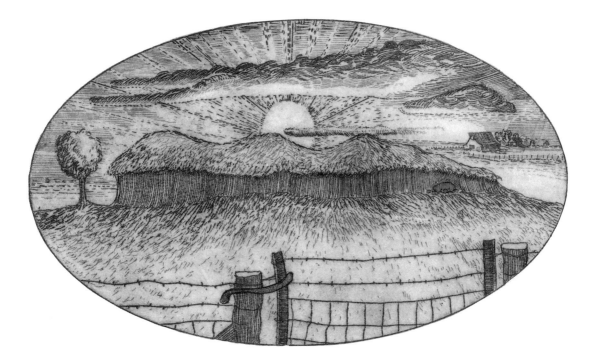

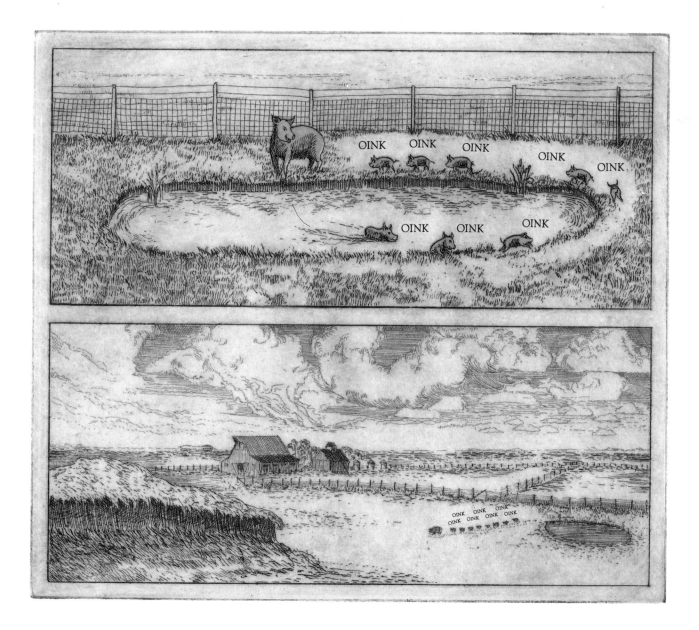

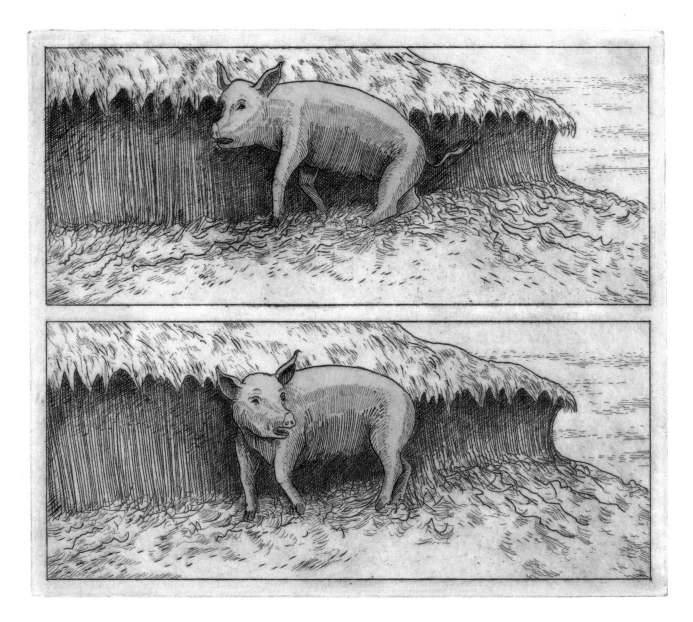

OINK